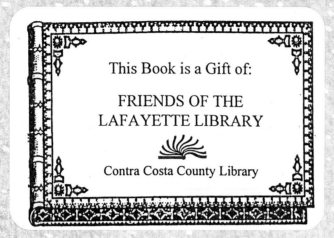

On Christmas Eve

PETER COLLINGTON

Alfred A. Knopf ⟶ New York

*This book is dedicated to
chimneyless children everywhere.*

*This is a Borzoi Book
published by Alfred A. Knopf, Inc.*

Copyright © 1990 by Peter Collington.
All rights reserved under International and Pan-American Copyright
Conventions. Published in the United States by Alfred A. Knopf, Inc.,
New York. Distributed by Random House, Inc., New York.
Published in Great Britain by Heinemann Young Books, London.
The right of Peter Collington to be identified as author of this work
has been asserted by him in accordance with the Copyright,
Designs and Patents Act 1988.
Printed in Scotland
First American Edition

2 4 6 8 10 9 7 5 3 1

Library of Congress Cataloging-in-Publication Data
Collington, Peter. On Christmas Eve.
Summary: Dozens of tiny fairies guide Santa Claus to the
home of a little girl who lives in a house without chimney.
[1. Christmas—Fiction. 2. Fairies—Fiction.
3. Stories without words] I. Title.
PZ7.C6860n 1990 [E] 90-4202
ISBN 0-679-80830-2 ISBN 0-679-90830-7 (lib. bdg.)

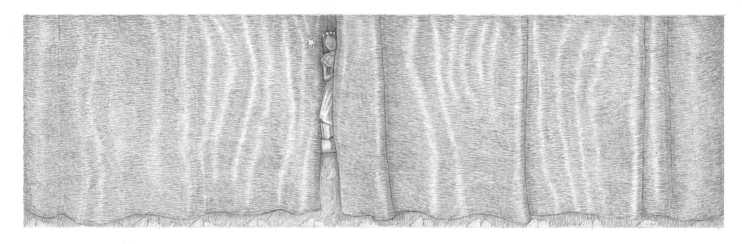

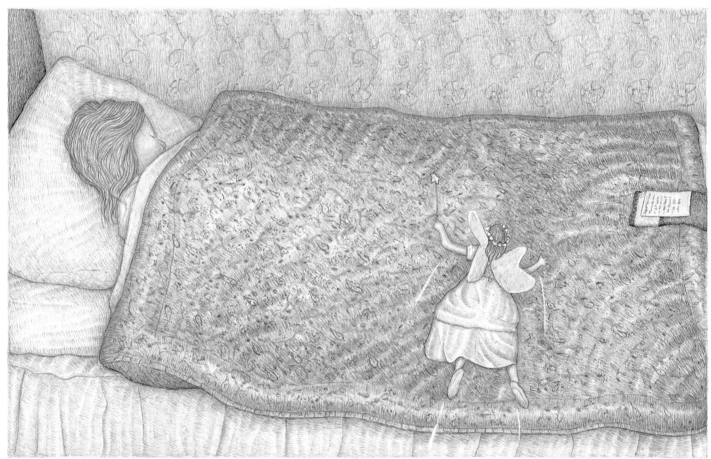

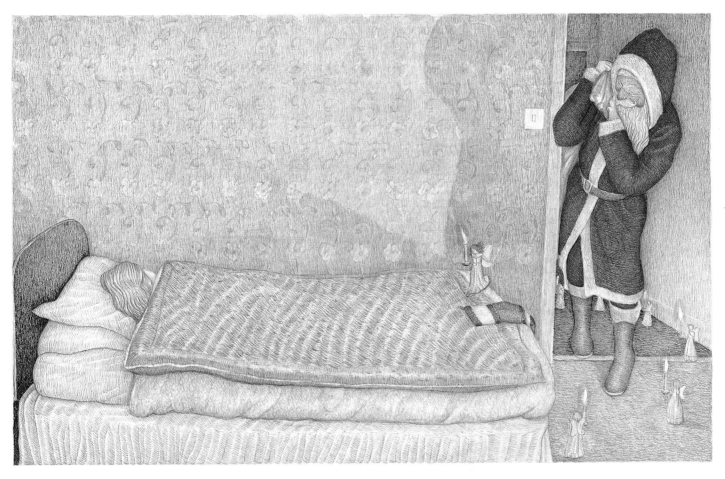

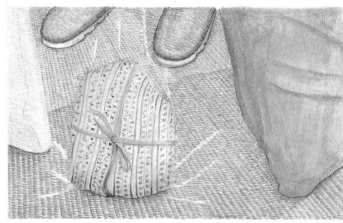

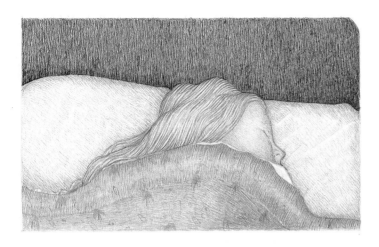

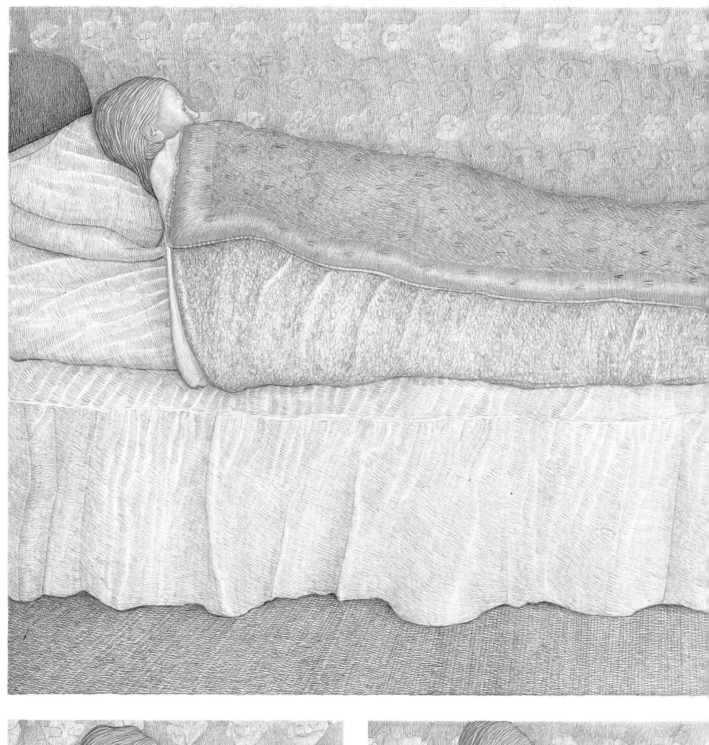

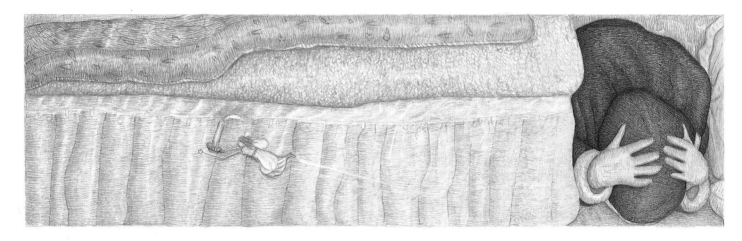

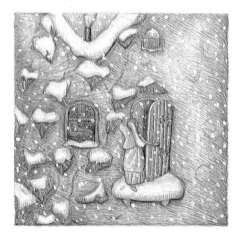